THE

GRONOX

WARS

Through the Ashes

The Gronox Wars

by Marilynn Dawson

CREDITS

Isaiah Dawson – Originator and owner of the space-fairing race presented within this book's pages. This novel and others in this series are being written for Isaiah by Marilynn Dawson – author and Isaiah's Mother. Cover art paid for by Colton W. Created by AlaisL.

Thank you to my beta readers for your valuable feedback: Zenanraptor720 Shannon and jboy22002.

Table of Contents

CHAPTER ONE: RESCUE OPERATION!

Sirens sounded in the carrier's hanger as announcements came thick and fast over the data waves!

"Another planet's been destroyed by the Gronox invasion fleet! Scramble the rescue ships! Toshang! Marshan! Man your ships and get the heck out of here!"

Toshang and Marshan, who had been on break discussing the upcoming coupling ceremony, jumped to their feet and raced to the marshaling platform.   Climbing into their combat suits, their respective crews arrived already suited up and racing on board to prepare the ships for launch. Some ran to the cargo bays situated in each wing of the refitted frigates. Those cargo bays were launching bays for stingers when the war had first begun, (stingers are tiny fighters no bigger than a scout vessel). Other crew took off to the cargo bays situated beneath the engine compartment and nose of the ships. Cilia, huge 3ft long fully-bendable tubes, rose from every inch of the frigates' exterior, giving the rescue vessels a "fuzzy" or "furry" look. Other crew dispersed through the two ships fitting out the med-bay, galley, and beginning preparations in the hidden bridge for take-off.

Time truly was of the essence before any further Shatong colonies fell to the oncoming Gronox flotilla. The Shatong had never encountered this type of warfare before. Space-faring life for them had been quiet up to this point, peaceful colonization was much preferred to the civil wars that nearly wiped them out centuries before. Now, whoever these Gronox were, they were shooting first and who knew when or if the alien race would stop to ask questions.

Toshang was the first to have his ship ready and exiting the air lock. Admiral Toshan came over the data wave with explicit orders, "Commander Toshang, you are to head straight to the Sharon system! Three planets there need immediate evacuation!"

"Rodger that" Toshang quipped, slamming the cilia hard down on one side to make a quick bank and bolt toward a safe exit zone. Perhaps one should pause a moment to understand a little of how Shatong vessels navigate the stars. The Shatong have patterned their technology after the wildlife they hunt and live among at home. Their space-faring vessels are powered and navigated by cilia much the way cilia allows one-celled organisms to move in the water of your own world. The undulating nature propels the ship forward, and flattening one group of cilia will cause the propelling action of other groups to move around it, thus turning the vessel this way or that in any direction at the whim of the navigator on board.

Commander Toshang sped toward his exit point. Deploying the forward sail, he shot the projectile into the sail, creating the vortex required to send his ship into hyperspace. Commander Marshan just shook her head as she dodged her way through the halls of her vessel up to the bridge. The ever-present understanding that her rescue vessel was much larger than Toshang's constantly meant he was forever out the gate before she could even issue the command to enter the airlock! Just once, she'd love to design her own ship where commanders had a secret passageway to the bridge! Upon entering the bridge, she assumed full squat position, plugged her tail tip into the system and was off!

Mere seconds upon leaving the airlock, Admiral Toshan was on the data waves again. "Commander Marshan, you are to head straight to Ponash and rescue as many colonists as you can before the Gronox arrive!

If we have their speed of advance calculated correctly, Ponash will be hit within hours! MOVE!"

Commander Marshan plugged in coordinates as fast as her thoughts would let her, deployed her sail and sent out the projectile before realizing she'd just aimed at a small asteroid! Too late! She fired off into hyperspace as Admiral Toshan watched the asteroid explode into a million tiny fragments.

"Extend the cilia!", "Cilia extended sir, we are passing through the shower unscathed." "Remind me to have another talk with Commander Marshan when she returns", "Ai, Sir".

Hyperspace was a busy place as Toshang and Marshan sped toward their respective coordinates.   Other rescue ships were coming back broadcasting tales of woe as they raced to rescue their kindred before the Gronox could wipe them out. Some of the rescue ships to the shrinking front line had not made it in time, suffering the same fate as the colonies they had been sent to rescue.

Toshang came out of hyperspace right above the first of the three planets he had to rescue in the Sharon system. Without even waiting for orders, five of his crew ran for the rescue pods and rushed to the surface. Toshang ordered remaining crew to prepare bunks and food for the Shatong about to be brought on board and made his way to the air locks.

Marshan dropped out of hyperspace on the dark side of a planet in the Ponash system and had her girls out of their airlocks and descending to the planet in record time. Not one to stay behind, she exited her rescue pod on the ground and became instantly bombarded by frightened and dazed Shatong of all ages and societal roles. A pregnant mother with three children suddenly came down with The Mother's Curse apparently as Gronox vessels came within a hair's breadth of discovering life on that planet. She ran up to Marshan in tears, begging for rescue. Marshan hurried her and the young ones inside, then stepped out to survey the colony. This would be the first time anyone ever heard of "The Mother's Curse" afflicting a woman in fear.

Her Privates and Captains continued to scramble the locals into the rescue pods when Marshan chanced upon the fallout. The Gronox HAD been here, but for some reason hadn't wiped out the colony. She turned tail and raced back to her pod, ordering all other rescue pods to leave the planet surface immediately! They'd only managed to salvage roughly half the colony as they rose back to her ship and docked inside.

"Decontamination crew to the airlocks immediately! Decontamination crew to the airlocks immediately! ALL crew and civilians to be scanned on arrival, myself included! NOW!"

A young man rushed up to Marshan as she exited her pod, waving a wand around her. When no warning lights emitted signals, she flattened out and tore up the hall to the bridge! Calculating an exit point aimed straight at the planet, she deployed the sail, shot the projectile and raced back into hyperspace for home.

A young private on the bridge turned around, "Uh, Ma'am? You do know that exiting aimed at a planet will destroy what remains of the colony?" Commander Marshan nodded her head, crunching her green eyes closed as she prepared to relay her findings to the Admiral and General Shanto. When she thought she could communicate without garbling the message, she plugged in her tail tip and began transmission.

"Sirs. . ." the message began, "My mission has only been partially successful. I have seen things today that I never want to see again. Homes looking like they got eaten alive. Bodies laying in their exposed beds, looking like decomposed maggots. (Language referring to the fact the Shatong was not yet dead. Their bodies turn to ash when they die.) A strangely-coloured acid-like substance unlike anything we Shatong have ever created oozing along stone surfaces but burning quickly through Shatong technology! Sirs. . ." She paused, trying to calm her trembling form, "Whatever this weapon is, it is fast-moving and extremely deadly!" She pulled out her tail tip and began to heave with sobs.

Her crew members had never seen the mighty Marshan in tears before and silently melted out of the room, focusing their attention on the rescued civilians instead. Marshan did her best to pull herself together as the ship came out of hyperspace and prepared to dock with the carrier. A messenger met her in the airlock with summons to the meeting room.

Toshang's rescue mission went much more smoothly. Crew members and civilians loaded rescue pods in orderly fashion to get as many on board as quickly as possible. Children carried babies while parents brought food rations for themselves and others with nothing. By the time all three planets were evacuated, Toshang's vessel had to navigate hyperspace at a much slower pace coming home. There had been no sign of the Gronox fleet anywhere in or near the Sharon system.

Commander Marshan stopped into her quarters to wash up quickly before facing the General and the Admiral. Upon entering the meeting room, she was immediately ushered to her place by the Admiral's aide.

"Sit down Commander." Admiral Toshan said as he appeared to be organizing information on his console. Marshan moved to an empty space at the table, folded her ample legs beneath her - assuming the female resting squat, and plugged in her tail tip. Shatong women, it must be noted, are several feet taller than their male counterparts. The hips and thighs of a Shatong female then, dictate that a chair or bench will cause stress and discomfort when she tries to sit down in the "normal manner". She must squat instead. Male Shatong on the other hand, with thighs and hips not quite so sizable, can make use of chairs and benches. Morphing back her helmet, (she had not yet shed her combat armour) she nodded to the others around the table-like structure that rose in the middle of the room. Admiral Shanto sent the required data stream to cause the table to morph viewing screens in front of each of the meeting participants.

"First things first Commander." Toshan began. "Please explain your exit behaviour earlier today."

Marshan mentally clopped herself upside the head. "I'm sorry sir. My focus was so much on the colony at Ponash that I failed to register the small asteroid directly in front of my vessel. It won't happen again sir. Was any damage sustained as a result of my negligence?"

5

"No Commander, we did not sustain any damage, however, Ponash apparently has, for the same reason Commander?" Admiral Toshan looked at her with an expression that read part quiz, part knowing and part scolding. "Please share with the General what you found."

General Shanto's attention went from Admiral Toshan to Commander Marshan's uneasy face and fidgeting hands. His deep voice quietly filled the room, "Commander?"

Somehow, Marshan took comfort from the sound of General Shanto's voice and her trembling quieted down. "Sirs, I bring grave news. Reports from Ponash had not been entirely accurate Sir," looking at General Shanto. "The outpost had stated the Gronox fleet had not come near the planet, only passed through the system, but that's not what I found on the planet surface."

Marshan sent information through her tail to the table's displays showing images of what she'd seen. The devastation of one area in the colony was almost complete. The infection however, was moving quickly as she sent image after image to the displays until she came to the image of the child in their bed.

General Shanto snapped his bright-blue eyes away from the display and plucked out his tail tip. "I wish I could block these images from my databanks! This is horrible! I knew the Gronox were using weaponry on a mass scale that was wiping out our colonies, but I had no idea it was this. . . this. . . infection or whatever it is!" Shanto's voice went from horror to anger as he slammed his fist on the table, causing all displays to briefly recalibrate. "Admiral Toshan, who is your best covert ops! Send them out behind enemy lines immediately! We MUST learn what this weapon is and FAST! Before it wipes out our entire race!"

Marshan looked nervously from Shanto to Toshan then began studying the Burgundy scales on the back of her hand. She was jolted out of her attempted momentary isolation by a data wave from Admiral Toshan demanding that she and Toshang return to her ship immediately to head out behind enemy lines. In shock, she rose up from her place, her facial scales a little paler than normal. She bowed to the two men, nodded to the aide, and quickly left the room.

CHAPTER TWO: AWAY TEAM

Toshang was just coming out of hyperspace when the message came over the data waves. Calling over his second-in-command, Toshang barked, "As soon as we dock, you are in charge of disembarking all passengers safely and into quarantine to be examined by the decontamination team! Once all passengers and crew have left the ship, you are to engage post-docking checklists and get this vessel ready for its next deployment. I will not be commanding the next rescue mission so I must leave you in charge." First Mate Goshan nodded and ran off to fulfill his duties.

Hurrying through the carrier's halls toward Marshan's vessel, the two nearly ran into each other coming around a corner near his quarters.

The carrier had been built to handle delivery of large numbers of frigates to key battle positions. Only four of these vessels were created after it was discovered that the spawning pools necessary to build them nearly took over the planets they'd been placed on. From space, each carrier looked like a large flat egg covered top and bottom with cilia, with rows of launch and cargo bay doors along the sides. The halls that Toshang and Marshan now ran down were tall, wide, and could accommodate a female at full height not to mention two side by side, or four male Shatong side by side. The walls and floors were reminiscent of the plant-based homes they lived in down on their home worlds. Their behaviour was the same as well, allowing for the health of the vessel to be maintained as well as that of it's occupants.

"Looks like we'll have time to finish plans for the coupling ceremony enroute to risk our lives for our people huh?" Toshang commented to Marshan as they untangled their tails and picked up their pace now running side by side toward her ship.

"Very funny Toshang. . ." Marshan dodged a private, "Planning our coupling while our entire race is in jeopardy!"

Toshang nearly ran over a food cart as he retorted, "But what if we're the only ones left when this battle is over? If we don't complete the coupling, who will carry on the mighty and peaceful Shatong?"

The two commanders entered the hanger and Marshan barked several orders to privates milling about before responding again. "Well," She half-smiled, "When you put it that way. . ." She gave Toshang's navy-blue hand a squeeze then shifted into command-mode. "Commander Toshang, your job will be to get us behind enemy lines. My job will be to intercept signals as outlined by High Command after the last skirmish where we learned how the Gronox communications work. If required, I will pretend we are Gronox having taken over a Shatong vessel. Nevermind that they would kill themselves trying to pull off such a feat, but they may be so hungry for a piece of our technology they may just fall for it. Once behind enemy lines, we need to find evidence of this weapon and bring it back to High Command."

"Yes, Ma'am!" Toshang responded and headed straight for the bridge. Marshan quickly walked a line of female warriors all hoping to be picked for the mission. She needed a scouting team with elite combat skills in case things went sideways in space or on the ground. Typically, soldiers specialized in one or the other, but just now, she was pleased to be examining a line of warriors who could fight both battles. She picked five women and assigned the remainder to Toshang's rescue vessel instead. It must be noted that Commander Marshan was a decorated warrior and gilded huntress in the annual Great Hunt.

To serve under her was in itself, a badge of honour.

Toshang himself was no one's slouch when it came to battle prowess or effectiveness in the Great Hunt. His ability to know where the enemy or prey were at any given time was uncanny, but while he'd been offered numerous promotions to Admiral, occasionally even being offered the position of General without having passed through the Admiral role, he routinely turned them down. His place was at the helm of a space-faring vessel or tapping into navigation signals on the ground. He was perfectly at ease in both locations and could not conceive of delegating the role to anyone else. Two of the female warriors looked forward to learning his tactics as they served under him on the bridge.

A private ran up to Marshan, "Ma'am, the galley is stocked for 3 weeks if we should need to be gone that long. The brig is cleaned up if we need to use it. The bunks are prepped and the ship's cilia have been thoroughly cleaned and made ready for the slightest feather touch in navigation. Is there anything I have missed Ma'am?" Marshan smiled at the private's report.

"Only one, Private. Please ensure we have a decontamination crew, quarantine crew, and containers both small and large to hold whatever we may find to bring back to High Command. I expect to be able to grab whichever size I need at the moment I need it."

The Private took off, sending out the required procurement order to Supplies and calling in the best crews he knew would please "the Mighty Marshan".

Marshan went to her private quarters to await word that all was ready for departure. As she passed by the mirror, she stopped and looked at herself, trying to envision what she might smell like as a pregnant mother. (Shatong babies are too small to make a Mom "look" prego, but a Mom's chemical signature changes instead) She liked to think she'd make a pleasant prego, provided The Mother's Curse didn't strike! That last vestige from the Shatong civil war would remain to plague Shatong women forever. Why oh WHY had they been so proud as to think that DNA manipulation would make them invincible, immortal, even fit to rule the galaxy?! The purists had been right after all, and if they hadn't won . . . Marshan shuddered, knowing if they hadn't won, she wouldn't be standing here today. But that was 300 years ago now! Yet to this day, The Mother's Curse could strike at any time! If they won this battle, if the Shatong survived, Marshan vowed to herself that she'd retire and become the best Mom any Shatong child could dream of! But. . . that required coupling and this blasted war just HAD to spring up JUST as she and Toshang thought they could spend the rest of their lives together! She grumbled as she climbed into her combat suit. Maybe she would give birth to the Shatong that would end The Mother's Curse once and for all. She tapped into her room's system just in time to receive the "all systems go", and raced to the bridge.

Toshang piloted the rescue ship out of the airlock and prepared for hyperspace. Studying charts and signals that had been received over the past 24 hours, he plotted a course, deployed the sail, and entered hyperspace. Now it was time to debrief the crew.

Opening a local data transmission port, Toshang began, "Warriors and Crew aboard the Rescue Vessel Leshad, you have been chosen for this mission because you are in the top five of your rank in the position you have been placed in. Whether you analyze the food being prepared, bandage wounds and dissect infections in the sick bay, man away teams or keep engines running, you are here because only the BEST would do!" A couple privates in the engine room giggled quietly. "We are on a top secret mission from High Command to go behind enemy lines!" The five warriors on board began to tremble with excitement! "All communication outside this vessel is restricted as of now, until we have completed our mission! Anything of an urgent or emergency nature must pass through myself or Commander Marshan for approval to be sent back to Shatong space. We must keep a low profile not only on Gronox radar, but also on the level of noise and chatter we generate. I have laid out a path that should take us through currently sparse Gronox territory, thanks to current incoming data transmissions. Please go about your duties only using the internal Shatong data waves until further notice."

One of the young female aces on the bridge nearly burst out in excitement had it not been for the glare coming from Toshang's orange eyes. She quickly composed herself and prepared to come out of hyperspace at the prescribed coordinates.

Marshan looked at the passage of time, wondering just how close to High Command the front line had come. She sent the order to prepare for landing the party, rose and left the bridge.

As Marshan joined her warriors in the airlock, waiting for Toshang to catch up, she struck up conversation with one nearby.

"So tell me Tishona, how did you become one of the best in the fleet?"

Tishona was adjusting her suit of armour and hooking up her hand-rifle when Marshan broached the question. The hand-rifle kind of looks like an old-fashioned jousting hilt at first, till one observes that the spear-like protrusion contains openings for clips holding a few acid rounds. The rifle is fired from within the hilt-like portion of the weapon.

"I managed to survive the attack on my colony, fending off a wave of tiny Gronox fighters. My fighter got blown up, but the force of the explosion actually threw me away from the vessel and toward a Shatong frigate. I grabbed some of the cilia and rode the frigate back behind the planet. I was able to find a air lock and crawl inside and we dove into hyperspace to escape the battle."

Toshang arrived and they entered the landing pod. As they entered the atmosphere around the planet, Tishona continued. "I was sent into battle a second time, this time near the Minash System. I was told to protect a transport rescuing civilians off the planet. I had to actually land on the planet and take on hordes of Gronox on the ground. They are so short!"

Marshan had to chuckle at Tishona's observation of their height. Toshang wasn't following the conversation, actively taking readings on the way down. Neither the nearby region of space, nor the planet seemed to have any sign of life or technology. Considering this was supposed to be a former Shatong colony, the lack of any signal at all put Toshang on the alert. Tishona and the others, picking up on his body language, readied their weapons and waited.

11

"Flanesh, What's your story?" Marshan asked as she turned to another Shatong warrior.

Flanesh briefly flushed as her hero addressed her. "My story is similar to Tishona's, but my colony got wiped out. I was so filled with shock and anger that my commander claims I took out five of their fighters in a blind rage!"

"That had to be SOME blind rage there Flanesh!" Dofeshi commented, checking to be sure weapons levels where sufficient if they got ambushed on the surface. Marshan silently observed Dofeshi as they all braced for landing.

The pod landed with a soft thump, sending clouds of ash up into the air. One warrior instructed the pod to gather an air sample. The air was breathable, but barely. They would need their suits to make up the slack. The group exited the pod unprepared for what would greet them. Grey skies overshadowed a blackened landscape where the colony had once stood. Blackened spires that hardly resembled the trees they once were, dotted the ground. A strong wind whipped through the area – a twister viewable in the distance, such weather no longer being hindered or tempered by tall, lush, green foliage. For a moment everyone stood there stunned.

CHAPTER THREE: THE GRONOX

Suddenly, seemingly out of nowhere, the little seven-man away team was ambushed by a ragtag band of Gronox ground forces all trying to get a shot off before closing in on hand-to-hand combat. The Gronox were a cybernetic race, as ruthless as they were expressive. Each Gronox was given full rein to enhance their abilities any which way they chose. The non-negotiables included the customary transmission and control chip in the brain, nano-bots to boost strength and speed, and the customary built-in arm rifle with it's accompanying energy round generation pack. The band of Gronox charging at the Shatong just now, were so covered by cybernetic implants and attachments as to nearly render their shape a lumpy, formless, moving mass. Only the resemblance of faces, arms, legs and feet could be adequately discerned. As to how exactly the actual race itself looked beneath the artificial facade, none of the Shatong could tell, if indeed anything was left biologically at all.

Marshan took a shot square in her chest, causing her to back up a step. The energy weapon's plasma breached the leather plating of her armour, but only for a moment as the membrane underneath re-spawned more leather to take its place. Seeing the short-lived gaping hole, one Gronox ran straight for her!

Marshan, who easily stood four to five feet taller than the Gronox soldier, stretched up to full height and uncoiled her thick, long tail. Snapping it around the soldier, she jerked him up into the air and with a sharp twist, sent him flying against a rock. Both lizard-like genders in the Shatong race have large tails, wide at the base spanning both hips and up to the small of the back. Their tails, often loosely coiled, can stretch out to at least double the average height of a Shatong's body. The coiled nature of their tail allows them to use it for a variety of purposes, including ground battle.

Another Gronox lost his cybernetic life support as Tishona's left claw's tore away a large panel followed in swift succession by her right claws' ripping cables, tubes and wiring from his back. Two Gronox tried to attack Toshang, thinking he was more their size, only to be picked up and slammed on the ground, the force of which killed them on impact. In truth, male Gronox are only 2/3'rds the height of Shatong females, so it is reasonable to consider that these two dead Gronox had figured a Shatong only a couple feet taller than themselves would be an easier target.

Toshang now knew why no signal of this rapidly-diminishing party had been picked up by his instruments. The ash-carrying wind was continually scattering any signal his suit was trying to relay to his brain. This same gale-force wind had earlier caused the Gronox platoon to crash-land on the planet, knocking out ship transmission capabilities.

One Gronox, upon trying to exit the damaged vessel, had been plucked up by the wind and tossed against a low-lieing stone retaining wall, rendering him unconscious. Unable to call for help or reinforcements, the remaining platoon members had carried out their mission to ensure no Shatong remained alive in the settlement, then had fallen into an uneasy sleep not far from their unconscious buddy.

Unbeknownst to the others, the unconscious soldier came to in a dream, kicking and screaming blue murder back on his home world. Deranged walking piles of weapons and wires were ordering every able-bodied young man onto the transports. But he would not go willingly. A grotesque humanoid shape reached out and clocked him in the head. He woke up on the operating table as the transmission chip was being inserted into his skull where the bone would keep it in place. Tendrils had been carefully inserted into brain soft tissue in strategic places to control his actions and words. . . or so they thought! Gromin tried to regain control of his hands, only to discover that one had gone missing while the other was now some sort of weapon! Roaring off the operating table, Gromin fought his way out of the so-called med-bay accidentally kicking another Gronox in real life, and began tearing through the transport as his dream continued. Gronox transformation techs smiled. It would only be a matter of time before the new recruit would see the benefits of his enhancements and begin to customize them to his liking. Realizing the futility of his efforts to find an escape pod, Gromin instead found an empty cot and pouted. The transmissions in his head were telling him to augment his suit with this weapon and that life-saving device, but he ignored them. When four cyborgs picked him up and threw him into a landing pod, transmission signals boosted to such strength that he could not overpower them. He'd just been pressed into active duty, his first mission being to ensure that the planet below was rid of its inhabitants.

The soft landing of the Shatong pod woke the Gronox troupe. To Gromin, it was merely a stranger sounding landing than what their own pod had made, causing the sound to stay within the bounds of his dream, failing to wake him. It would be the sounds of unsuccessful hand-to-hand combat and the firing of weapons that would rouse the unwilling Gronox from his troubled dream.

Groggy eyes observed the skirmish from behind the stone retaining wall. He winced as a fifth platoon comrade lost his life at the hands of the Shatong. The ease with which the Shatong soldiers were dispatching his platoon mates caused him to briefly turn away from the scene, close his eyes and slump against the wall. Truly, if the new weapon had not been discovered, all the Shatong would have to do is bring the battle to the ground and they would win. Their speed, height, and strength were no match for a Gronox soldier on the ground.

When the sounds of fighting had ceased, Gromin opened his eyes again to find two Shatong standing not far from him, stock still. Their helmeted heads were looking just past him and not even their tails appeared to move.

Gromin followed their gaze to the ground where he was laying. A struggling sample of the same ooze-like substance Marshan had seen on Ponash, was trying to approach the soldier across the large flag-stones, but kept retreating.

Gromin struggled to his feet, the transmission chip no longer functioning and his limbs seemingly unsure how to respond to his own commands. "Kill me and you'll never learn why I and my comrades did not die of this infection. I am worth more to you alive than dead!" Those were brave words coming from a slightly-disoriented and rebellious Gronox. After all, he himself did not know what this infection was nor why it would not attack him.

Infection??? Marshan would have flown at the soldier in blind rage had Toshang not touched her arm. "Disarm yourself first, soldier!" Toshang barked.

Gromin pulled out his plasm pack and tossed it at Toshang's feet. Holding up his hands to show cybernetic weapons aimed away from the Shatong duo, he walked slowly toward them, face full of rebellious defiance. His race had been conquered once, he'd been misshapen once, whatever these towering lizards were going to do couldn't be any worse. He'd take it like the young man he'd been taught to become. Marshan used her tail to spring behind him and clapped his "hands" together over his head as Toshang began figuring out why the young man had not called for reinforcements. Just then, the other warriors returned, having gathered various ash samples from what used to be the town square.

A few quick codes over the data waves and the team was headed back to the pod with their prisoner. Inside, Gromin studied the floor, Dofeshi and Shateena squatting on either side of him to ensure nothing would happen. Marshan and Toshang studied him, curious why there seemed to be more of a humanoid form with him than with the others.

"Where are you from young man?" Toshang enquired "You do not look like a typical Gronox."

"I am NOT a Gronox!" the young man retorted. "The Gronox captured my race apparently while in battle with you guys! I refused to assimilate!"

Youthful eyes tried hard to focus on the grainy lines in the floor. A firmly clamped but quivering lip caused Marshan to feel sorry for the young man. Shateena looked as if she wanted to put an arm around the young prisoner, but instead studied a glove-enforced left talon.

"But you did assimilate." Marshan said quietly. At that the young man's face shot up to look her square in the eye.

"The chip they put in my brain gave me almost no choice! That thing controlled how I moved, where I went, and even tried to control what I say!" The words barely escaped his mouth when he realized. . . "Wait a minute. . . I'm saying my own thoughts!" Dismay, wonderment, and a look that suggested potential hope from stiffening despair caused Toshang to rise from his seat. The two warriors pulled out scanners and relayed the data to Toshang.

Everyone went silent as the pod docked with the Leshad.

Both the quarantine and decontamination crews met them in the airlock.

As soon as Toshang could, he grabbed the sample vials, including one with a small trace of the live "infection" as the soldier had called it, and ran to the lab, barely getting the vials into containment before the trace began trying to eat its housing. After instructing the lab tech to boost containment, he raced to the bridge to make his report.

Marshan was already there intercepting a distress call and plotting coordinates.

"NO! We have to get back to base!"

Marshan calmly but firmly planted both feet, placed her hands on her hips and replied, "The Leshad is a rescue vessel! We will rescue our people wherever we find them on our way back! I couldn't save my colony! I couldn't rescue all of Ponash! I MUST try to rescue what's left of Tomashi! I swear Toshang, if this war renders me subjected to The Mother's Curse, I want the satisfaction of knowing I rescued as many of our people as I could!"

"But what if this unsanctioned mission causes our own vessel to lose containment? That live sample could kill us all and then proceed to wipe out every last Shatong! What will your bravery do then?"

Marshan paced a moment, "We Shatong believe in the importance of life! We are descendants of the Purists, Toshang! The Purists refused to allow our race to become like the Gronox!"

"Like the Gronox?" Toshang repeated, crossing his arms over his chest as he better positioned himself to listen.

"Like the Gronox!" Marshan resumed. "The Progressives wanted free reign to genetically modify themselves however they deemed fit. They wanted to be stronger, faster, bigger, smarter, and to build in whatever designer qualities at conception that they so desired! Toshang its in the bloomin' history books! Designer children! How disgusting can you get?! It's precisely because of the attempt to create the ability for any Shatong mother to design her own baby that we've been stuck with The Mother's Curse ever since! Our researchers still can't find the reproductive gene that got tampered with by the Progressives, nor can they predict when it will strike or under what conditions and it's been over 400 years since that civil war! If we are going to be wiped out, we will be wiped out pure! If we are going to survive, we will survive pure! Either way, I MUST answer this distress call!"

CHAPTER FOUR: GROMIN

Toshang knew that tangling with Marshan when her mind was made up, was not wise. He sighed, wondering what base command would do this time and busied himself with his report. It was his turn to be surprised at the speed of transport a while later as the call went through the ship, "Man the stingers!"

Toshang exited the bridge, nearly getting run over by three aces on their way to cargo bay three. The hallways of a frigate are not as large as those of the carrier. Frigates built for female warriors were larger than those built for Shatong male warriors, that's true. But space was at a premium regardless. Time seemed to go in slow motion as Toshang watched a string of pods follow Marshan to the surface. It appeared that his hoped-for bride was observing his report as he wrote it, because the stingers hardly got into striking distance before they began shooting their acid weapon at the ground, creating a dead zone the infection could not pass surrounding one wing of the settlement. Shatong streamed into this zone as fast as they could with Marshan directing medical personnel to load the pods to overflowing. Pods began racing to and from the planet until Marshan's team was forced to leave due to the infection having followed a root into the safe zone. She managed to save most of the colony that day, but not before nearly collapsing as she left the airlock for the final time. Toshang ushered her to the mess hall for some much-needed and overdue nourishment. After only two legs of meat, Marshan threatened to nod off in her food. Excusing herself, she got up and stumbled off to bed. Even the "Mighty Marshan" couldn't go more than two days without sleep.

Returning to Shatong space, Toshang headed back to base. Toshang now had his own mission to accomplish. Marching down to the High Command meeting rooms, he pushed aside the two guards and entered without knocking, straight into an off-world meeting of top Shomadeer officials. Admittedly, General Shanto had said nothing of hosting Shomadeer leaders on this particular carrier at this particular time. Toshang was not at all sure he liked the idea of Shatong Shomadeer anywhere but back on the home world where they would hopefully stay safe.

All eyes turned to the meeting's intruder as Commander Toshang strode quickly to the middle of the room. "Sirs, I am Commander Toshang of the 4th Fleet. I come with terrible news!" Toshang made a quick glance meeting eye to eye with each Shomadeer member as he thrust his tail tip into the floor. Stopping his gaze on the Shatong High Governor, Toshang issued the command to send the away team conversation with the Gronox prisoner to the desk of every Shomadeeror present.

"Not a true Gronox!" One jumped up and exclaimed.

"Captured?? The Gronox were capturing other races while seeking to annihilate us??" Another questioned.

A female Shomadeeror began to weep softly as she imagined what the parents of this young man must have gone through seeing him carted off.

Finally, General Shanto stood to his feet. "Commander Toshang, according to military and Shomadeer protocol, I should have you thrown in the Brig until this war is over!" Toshang swallowed, determined to share his message and hoping for leniency just this once. Shanto continued, "However, We will listen to your presentation before Shomadeer.

If it is deemed to be of urgent life-saving importance, your trip to the Brig will be commuted."

Toshang nodded, straightened up his armour and began, "Sirs, as per the information passed to you regarding the recent recon trip behind enemy lines, the Gronox are not above capturing members of other races and pressing them into service. It is my professional opinion and recommendation sirs, that our military requirement for all personnel serving in this war, be extended to ALL civilians!"

"Here, here!" a back-bench Shoma shouted.

An elderly Shatong Shoma wobbled to his feet, grasping a gnarled stick for support and placing his free hand on the desk in front of him. "We must never allow our technology, nor our knowledge of advanced genetics to get into the hands of other races! We have seen the devastation caused by this Gronox race, and now we have seen their ruthlessness. At no time must a soldier or civilian among us be taken captive, alive!" The effort required for the elderly gentleman to express such a string of sentiments meant he had to pause and sit down.

The Shatong High Governor now stood to his feet. "The commander brings timely advice. When coupled with our elder's thoughts on this matter, I hereby propose the following resolution." All eyes turned to his end of the room. "The destabilization packets issued to all soldiers, must now be issued to all civilians, to be worn under the same scale on the left shoulder, only to be activated when faced with imminent capture. Children too young to be trusted with not picking at their scales are to have their packets stored with their parents. All in favour raise their right hand!"

Slowly, right hands began to rise around the room, only a couple Shatong abstained.

The Shatong High Governor resumed, "20 to 2 in favour of this change in wartime policy. Let it be done!"

General Shanto became uneasy. He released an unwitting shudder through the room's data waves. Standing to his feet and slowly unplugging his tail from its port, he added, "Our children are our future, now perhaps more than any other time in Shatong history. However let it be noted that children imitate their parents, blurt things out when they shouldn't, and see far more than they are given credit for. It is for these reasons, and these reasons alone that I will follow Shomadeer orders. For any other reason I would ask to be relieved of duty rather than follow through on such a dire directive."

He walked to the centre of the room, put a hand on Toshang's shoulder, and ushered him out of the chamber.

A banging on Marshan's door woke her up. Falling out of bed, she grabbed the wall to steady herself as she rose to her feet and made her way to the door. With her green eyes still focusing, she answered the knock.

"Commander Marshan? Admiral Toshan is requesting your presence in the Brig"

Marshan nodded to the messenger, closed her door and went to wash up. She grabbed a small bit of jerky on her way out the door, checking the time as she left. Her eyes popped open when the clock read a full 12 hours since she and the Leshad had docked! After the meeting in the Brig, she needed to go find some food.

Arriving at the Brig, she found Admiral Toshan, Commander Toshang, General Shanto and several scientists all hovering over the lone Gronox soldier.

"What's your name!" General Shanto's deep voice boomed.

"Gromin. . . sir." Gromin replied. The Shatong seemed taller now than when he'd seen them on the planet! Even the Shatong men stood several feet above the tallest Gronox he'd ever seen!

"Gromin is it?" Toshang echoed. "and why have you not called in reinforcements? All that tubing and wiring and whatever it is entering and leaving your body seems rather silent beyond it's own operation."

Gromin held his head. "I have been trying unsuccessfully to call for help ever since you found me, but all I can manage is this horrible migraine!"

A scientist from the medical wing approached, scanning the Gronox soldier's head looking for abnormalities based on previous soldiers found dead and dissected to learn about this strange enemy. The scientist turned to Toshang and the others, "Sirs, Ma'am, he is unable to broadcast because the systems surrounding a damaged chip in his brain are unable to codify nor transmit the message he is trying to send out. For lack of better wording sirs, it appears our prisoner has brain damage."

General Shanto turned to Marshan, "Good work capturing one of the enemy alive, but you do realize such an action could have put your entire mission at risk?"

"Yes sir, I am aware, but when you saw what the infection was doing near him, you'll understand."

"Infection? Is that the term for this sample that was brought back?"

"Yes sir, Gromin himself referred to it as such."

Gromin nodded as General Shanto looked in his direction. Turning to Toshang, General Shanto ordered, "Toshang, get our research crew on those samples pronto! Planets are being lost. In the time you two were away, we lost four more planets to the Gronox and they have not stopped their advance! Time is of the essence and we MUST stop this new weapon!" Turning back to Gromin, General Shanto growled, "And you, mister prisoner, will be part of the research, whether you live or die."

The guards returned a scowling, angry Gromin to his holding cell as the entourage left the Brig.

Stopping the General, Marshan enquired, "Sir, were you not informed of this prisoner's true identity?"

23

"What, you mean that he was captured? That he was pressed into service? Did YOU hear him say that he'd been trying to call for help ever since you captured him?"

Marshan sighed. "Sir, the soldier is just a boy, a youth." She sent the image of Gromin's firmly clamped but quivering lip as he studied the floor. General Shanto frowned, scrunched his bright-blue eyes closed before opening them to walk faster up the hallway. Marshan stopped walking and let him move on.

Toshang carried the orders to the lab and the weapons scientists. Over the next few days, he and Marshan would be sent out on more rescue missions as the Gronox continued to push further and further into Shatong space. Planet after planet was rendered uninhabitable by this new weapon. Anxious to see how research was going, Toshang took leave of his vessel again and ran to the labs.

CHAPTER FIVE: THE WEAPON

"How much longer before you guys have something?! I keep checking the logs but nothing conclusive ever shows up! Do you guys know just how close to home world we are now???"

The research team straightened up at Toshang's questions. One approached, "Sir, with all due respect, we have not been able to discover why this infection would not attack the Gronox, only that it seems to act as if two magnetic poles were opposing each other. We have been unable to replicate this using our own systems. The research centres just won't do it. But. . ."

"But WHAT?! Lives are being lost throughout Shatong space! We NEED a counter weapon YESTERDAY!" Toshang thundered! One researcher quipped to another, "I think his roar is worse than the General's!"

The first researcher resumed speaking, "But as I was going to say sir, we have uncovered how the Gronox are able to fire this weapon while maintaining their invisible protection around their ships." Toshang was suddenly all ears, giving the younger Shatong his full attention.

"Say on. . ."

"Sir," the researcher resumed, "They have to modulate their . . . shields I think they call them?" Another researcher nodded affirmatively. "Yes, shields, to let the weapon through. They fire a projectile of sorts that enters a world's atmosphere and just sort of floats to the surface. When the infection lands on the surface, it goes after anything of a biological nature and destroys it. We've studied images of homes eaten alive, and the ashes of Shatong who have died, and they were all struck with this infection."

"So what's the answer then? How do we combat this?"

"We outfit our ships' weaponry to fire a re-engineered version of this weapon at their ships.."

"Hand me the data! We don't have time for further talk!"

The researcher plugged in his tail, Toshang slammed his into the floor, and the data was exchanged. As soon as the last bit passed through, Toshang was running down the hall toward the carrier's weapons tech, broadcasting over the data waves that a solution had been found!

Every weapons tech on board the carrier ran toward the main weapons research hub to get debriefed on the new attack weapon. Discussion hammered down to retrofitting the acid guns so that they could shoot either acid or infection at oncoming Gronox vessels. Weapons techs back on the home world took the specs and began drafting a prototype. During the building the of the prototypes, the weapons tech crew still aboard the carrier discovered what they began to call, "the kill switch". Testing it on the only sample of "infection" they had, it was effectively neutralized and killed. Word of the discovery was sent to Admiral Toshan as he sat with others in a meeting. His response sent the various weapons techs back on home world scrambling again to ensure the "kill switch" was built into each prototype, the concept being to activate it immediately after firing the new weapon against the Gronox.

They'd barely completed the prototypes and were preparing to do a test fire when word of a pause in the Gronox advance came to light.

Admiral Toshan wasted no time in picking up on the slowed Gronox activity, continually demanding updates to know how quickly the Shatong prototypes were being built. By the second full day of retrofits, he was pleased to learn that one complete prototype had been built and received their ammunition. Another prototype ship was almost done but had yet to receive their shipments while the last prototype ship was awaiting parts before it could be built. Shatong weapons techs worked around the clock with no rest to accomplish the feat. The lives of countless civilians hung in the balance.

Toshan called a meeting of his favourite covert ops and the General to compare notes, updates, and to take a collective breath. As the four Shatong entered their meeting room, sirens throughout military installations around the home world sounded, as data waves ordered every single weapons tech to man their stations! Medics were told to stand by and all unnecessary personnel were told to move into bunkers below the planet surface! Admiral Toshan punched in code to open a viewing port on the wall of the meeting room and the four watched in silence.

The largest Gronox fleet yet amassed, came out of hyperspace on the dark side of the planet. Sensors picked up their infection weapons aimed straight at the home world. The four planet-sized carriers now stationed around the home world scrambled their pilots and gunners. As wave after wave of fighters and frigates began exiting the carriers, the Gronox began firing at the planet! For a time, it appeared as if the Shatong fleet was actually fending off the infectious attack, blowing up the canisters while they were still in space. But the Gronox had only unleashed their first wave.

Suddenly it seemed as if the Gronox larger vessels were venting. On closer inspection however, that was no steam coming from their ships, rather, that was thousands of what the Shatong would have labeled Stingers, being launched to take on the Shatong fleet. The Shatong fighters and frigates once again proved to be no match for the Gronox forces, due in large part to the fact the Shatong did not have any technology even remotely related to the concept of shields.

Admiral Toshan messaged the home world research centres anxious to know if the prototypes were ready yet. As if in answer, sensors began picking up strange signals as Shatong weapons techs launched the prototypes into space. Shatong fighters were starting to lose in vast numbers when the prototypes began firing round after round of their own canisters at the surrounding ships, firing directly into clouds of Gronox fighters.. Gronox ships began to break off, creating their own exit points to get out of Shatong space! Some made it into hyperspace showing early signs of death throes as the "infection" began to eat away at anything that smacked of a biological nature. The prototypes immediately began firing their kill switch signals, testing whether or not such a signal would prevent the "infection" from changing course to attack the Shatong instead.

Aboard the Gronox flagship, a Gronox commander pounded his chair with his fists as he angrily shouted into the fleet intercom, "RETREAT! RETREAT! ALL SHIPS TO HYPERSPACE! DISENGAGE NOW!!!" Ship after ship began to behave erratically and then list off into uncontrolled spirals indicating all on board had perished.

What the Shatong High Command had not yet been told, was that as of this particular assault, all that was left of inhabitable Shatong space, was the home world! All other bases and stations orbited dead worlds or sat in empty space. The question now, was what drove off such a large armada! Why had they aborted their attack on the Shatong home world? And most importantly, why had the "infection" not turned around and attacked the Shatong itself after devouring life on so many other worlds?

The great research centres scattered around the home world went into high gear seeking answers to these questions. As discoveries were made, such as how the kill switch actually worked, High Command got antsy that the Gronox had not only gone quiet, not only quit advancing, but that this lull was lasting far too long. It was time for another excursion into enemy territory.

Admiral Toshan called in Toshang and Goshan. "Gentlemen, our sensor arrays have been unusually quiet for far too long. I want the two of you to make a scouting run into Gronox space and return with news of what you find."

"What about Marshan? She's good with covert missions, if the rescue ships get called out again, Goshan would be needed here."

"Marshan is undergoing reparative therapy as we speak, Toshang." The Admiral responded. "She is not fit to head back into enemy territory at this time."

Toshang's countenance fell. The Mighty Marshan in therapy! He knew the sights of the battle had taken a toll on her, but hearing she was in reparative therapy almost made him want to stay home. Slowly he stood up and commented, "Alright sir, Goshan and I will go."

Admiral Toshan nodded gravely as Goshan rose and the two men left the room.

As Toshang and Goshan sped through hyperspace in their tiny single-armed scout, readings continued to be quiet. The former chatter that filled the hyperspace channels was reduced to the hum of their own ship and the singing of the stars. Toshang made a point of stopping by every single signal emissions point en-route, with nothing showing up on the screen or in the data waves.

Dropping out of hyperspace at one system that had been clearly marked as Gronox territory before the war began, Toshang and Goshan gasped at the scene before them. A small fleet of Gronox ships looked like a proverbial dumping ground. Not wanting to attract attention, they re-entered hyperspace and headed for another system well within Gronox space. It must be noted that their scout vessel was not equipped with the infection's kill switch.

Again they dropped out of hyperspace at a fully-Gronox-held system and heard a perpetual repeating mayday coming from a space station near one of the planets. "Mayday, Mayday! 12-20-5032, 10-20-20, Something is eating our people and food stores! Get us off this station! Mayday! Mayday!" Goshan stopped the ship just inside the entry point as they listened to the message over and over again. Toshang began comparing logs he'd brought with him, dates, times, locations, transmissions. When the mayday was heard for the tenth time, Toshang sat bolt upright!

"Goshan, get us back into hyperspace NOW!" Goshan, taken by surprise, spun the vessel around, deployed the sail, shot the projectile and had the ship in hyperspace before Toshang could say another word. "Uh, Sir? Usually we enter hyperspace with a set of coordinates, but we're shooting off to who knows where now. Where should we be headed sir?"

Toshang motioned for home as he tried to calm himself down before sending sobering data ahead of them. "Goshan. . . that mayday took place a few days ago. The fact the message was not halted means no one came for them. Did you hear the whole thing? Something was eating their people and food stores! We had to get out of there before the infection learned of our presence!"

"Infection??? The one that was being used against our people? The one we built a kill switch against?"

"Yes Goshan, THAT infection!" Toshang continued to pour over the logs to find out just how the infection ended up ravaging Gronox space. One log entry captured the action of a battle ship retreating from the home world skirmish where the prototype had been fired. The crew were still alive as they'd left Shatong space. There was a long pause as the scout vessel made it's way through hyperspace toward home. The greying pensive look on Toshang's face was all Goshan needed to remain silent. Whatever was bothering his boss would be revealed only to the right people in the right places.

Toshang grimly wrote up his report and fired it off. Now he too was wishing command would send him into reparative therapy.

CHAPTER SIX: LOSS

A few hours later, back on the carrier, the halls were quieter than usual. Just as many Shatong made their way through the great ship to carry out their duties, but the hum over the data waves was muted, subdued, even sorrowful. As Toshang made his way to the Admiral's office, it was clear that word had gotten out of the fate of the Gronox race. He softly knocked on the Admiral's door, and it spiralled open unhindered.

The Admiral sat with his back to Toshang, head bowed and tail limp, though still connected to the data port. "Come in Commander." He said quietly. "You have brought back grave news for our people. We mourn like we've never mourned before." He slowly turned around as Toshang took his place. Goshan followed a few steps behind, not sure if he should enter. Toshang waved him off, that his presence was not needed, relieving him of duty for the moment to go and rest in his quarters. Goshan accepted the data wave and disappeared.

Toshang and Toshan sat in silence for several minutes. Each needing a moment to grieve over the loss of a race they'd hardly met or even gotten to know. The only living Gronox now sat in a holding cell in the Brig and when he died, there'd be nothing left.

Because Gronox do not communicate using biological systems, Gromin would be the only being in Shatong space to NOT know what had just occurred. It was time to pay him another visit.

Silently, Admiral Toshan led Toshang down to the Brig. Their bowed heads causing every Shatong they passed to pause to one side and lower their heads until they passed. One could be forgiven for thinking such a sight reminded them of the honour guard on their own world. Two high-ranking female warriors joined the procession, their tail tips touching their right shoulder as the only posture Shatong can assume when wishing to bow. They represented the fighter pilots who had flown the prototypes the day of the fateful log entry.

Two privates joined the entourage with empty food carts to pick up the gifts others had begun tossing in the way. Such behaviour was usually only reserved in solidarity with a Mother who had lost her unborn child, the gifts being intended to make life easier during her mourning period and healing after the stillbirth ceremony was completed. By the time the small parade had made it to the Brig, both food carts were overflowing and a third private had joined with a large sack that was now almost full.

The guard at the Brig's post needed no instruction, but immediately led the Admiral to Gromin's cell, then stood to one side to make room for everyone who had joined the procession. The Admiral motioned to the privates to bring forward the gifts. They did so and then they too went to stand by the prison guard. Gromin looked over the solemn and, dare he say, sad(?) group of Shatong before him.

Admiral Toshan cleared his throat and began, "Gromin, we are here to inform you that. . . that you are all that is left of your people." Admiral Toshan struggled to maintain composure. "Commander Toshang and I have come to express our deepest regrets at what has happened. It was not our intent to wipe out an alien race we'd barely just met, let alone such a race as would capture and forcibly enslave a race such as was yours. Please accept our gifts of condolence, and should the time come in the future, you will be free to live out your days among us as our honoured guest."

Honoured guest??? HIS people??? Gromin scratched a tube on his head. But the real Gronox tried to kill both of us! His thoughts got scrambled as he tried to make sense of the mourning he now understood before him. Nodding, he thanked the Admiral and began to pull the gifts into his cell. When the two carts and bag were all the way inside, the Brig guard strengthened the containment field again as the group hung their heads in silence for a moment longer. When the customary time had elapsed, beginning with the privates in reverse order to how they arrived, they left.

Toshan, Toshang, Shateena and Tishona were barely out of audible hearing range when they heard what sounded like cheering coming from the Brig. Looking at each other quickly, they spun tail and headed back. To their bewilderment, there was Gromin in his cell, practically dancing for joy, holding up a pair of snack bones as if they were trophies!

Gromin caught sight of the four Shatong as he spun about, and almost began laughing at their incredulous faces. "You look positively confused!" Gromin observed with a humorous tone to his voice.

Toshang responded, "Well, you are aware of what we'd just announced to you a few moments ago. In seeking to save our own race from extinction at the hands of the Gronox, we ended up wiping out their race. If what you told us in the pod on our way up from the blackened planet is true, that means your race was wiped out along with the Gronox, thanks to their having conquered your own race."

Gromin took a deep breath. "Well sir, my story is true, the Gronox did conquer my people and force us to assimilate into their empire. My people raise their children to have strong minds, which is why my assimilation was not complete. It is why I am not attacking you now as per the directives left in my head before the chip got damaged. You have rescued me from more than abandonment on a dead planet. You have liberated me from the Gronox as well, and THAT my friends, is cause for celebration! The Brig guard here says these sticks are used like candy to your people?" Gronox asked, brandishing a marinated blue stick. Toshan nodded.

"Then here!" Gromin tossed a handful of the bones to the four Shatong. The Brig guard had not been informed of this development and the two sticks bounced off the containment field back into the cell.

Tishona, standing behind the other three, received summons along with Dofeshi, to prepare for their next mission. She quietly bowed out of the Brig and ran to the cargo bays. When Marshan learned of it, she left her reparative therapy unit to man the third prototype herself. General Shanto wanted the kill switch sent to every single system logged inside Gronox space. Mop-up, if you will. After all that she had seen, there could be no better way to ensure such nightmares never occurred again, but by firing the kill signal herself at every granted opportunity!

The three prototypes left the home world, and in a show of mourning, slowly made their way to the farthest exit point in the system.

Toshang's visit with Gromin was interrupted to receive urgent communications from the home world hospital, pleading with him to make Marshan turn around and come back. She was in no condition to fight, they said, and would only make her condition worse if she encountered more horrors. Toshang took his time responding as he and Toshan left the Brig, knowing that each must mourn in their own way, and that Marshan needed closure. He opened a view port just in time to see the three prototypes disappear into the sail and begin their journey.

Shateena however, stayed behind in the Brig as the others left to attend to the urgent business at hand. "Corporal Damoshe", she addressed the Brig guard, "Could you let me inside Gromin's cell please?" Still dressed in her combat armour, Shateena was nothing to sneeze at, and the guard let her in without answering a word, resuming containment once she was fully inside.

Gromin backed out of the way, almost tripping over the gifts as he sat down on the cot.

"eh my young man, it's OK. I'm not here to hurt you. Did you know I had a son your age once?"

Gromin looked mildly surprised, "My age? How do you know my age? You don't know a thing about my people!"

Shateena smiled, "No Gromin, I don't know anything about your people, that's true, but I do know youth when I see and hear it. If I had to wager a guess, I'd place you around 15? Maybe 17?" She asked, slightly cocking her head to one side.

Gromin shifted his feet, "I'm almost 15. . . good guess. . ."

Shateena continued, "I lost my son when the Gronox invaded Nopeshi Prime. The rescue ships had come for us, but Zolash was out on one of his hunting quests. He was out of data wave range so I couldn't signal him to come home. I didn't want to leave without him, but my husband and relatives pushed me on-board the ship. He would have been 15 next month."

Gromin's eyes met hers as he quietly responded, "Sorry to hear of your loss. You must have loved him dearly. . ." at which he looked away, pretending to study another gift from the cart.

Shateena nodded, "He was my firstborn. My husband and I have three younger children who were all home that day, so they are now safe on the home world, thankfully." Shateena began to pick up vibes from the boy suggesting he might be tired and rose to leave. "I'll come visit you tomorrow OK?"

Gromin forced a smile. Hearing of her loss made it hard to maintain his tough exterior. He missed his family so badly! He nodded as he began digging through the gifts hoping to find something to hide the tears he'd shed as soon as she was gone.

Because the prototypes could only carry a set level of supplies, the mission had been told to keep each system's visit short, no more than a few hours in any given location to ensure the "infection" would not return. Mop-up was not without it's hiccoughs, as infected ships had begun to find "new life" so-to-speak as the infection had discovered systems it could use to further its hunt for food sources.

Occasionally, this meant dropping out of hyperspace and firing the kill signal at oncoming ghost-ships! It would be roughly a month by the time the women returned, gaunt, thinner than was healthy, and almost depressed to the point of being institutionalized by their loved ones.

CHAPTER SEVEN: HOPE

Shateena had kept her word and began making daily visits to Gromin's cell. She took over the role of bringing the noon meal so that she and Gromin could eat together. During one of their visits, Shateena got a communication from her husband down on the home world. Opening a view port in the holding cell's wall, she accepted the communication.

"Hi honey," Zomesh greeted Shateena. "Are those cell block walls I see behind you?"

Shateena laughed, "Why yes they are, my love! I have someone I wish to introduce you to." She motioned for Gromin to sit beside her.

"Well, well, well, "Zomesh commented, "Now who do we have here? What is your name young man?"

Trying to figure out how the view port seemed to just appear out of nowhere, Gromin brought his attention back to the subject in the screen and responded, "I'm Gromin."

"I've been visiting Gromin every day since we found him abandoned with other Gronox during a covert away mission two months ago.."

"The Gronox! What are you doing befriending the very race that tried to annihilate us!" Zomesh demanded!

Gromin began to get scared, nervously looking from the screen to Shateena to the floor.

"He's the same age as our Zolash and lost his entire race to the Gronox., he doesn't belong to the race that tried to wipe us out", Shateena quickly responded. There was an uneasy pause for a few moments, before the three children began trying to poke their heads into the viewing area.

Shateena's 12yr old daughter jumped right in front of her husband at one point, big yellow eyes bright."So when you coming home Momma? When you coming home?"

"Yeah! We, Want, Momma!" The two younger boys began to chant. "We, Want, Momma!"

Gromin found himself smiling at the younger Shatong children all trying to say hi to Mommy and ask questions at the same time. His smile wasn't lost on the parents.

"Alright Shateena, keep me posted on how the young man is doing. I'm sure High Command won't keep him in that cell for long."

Shateena smiled so big her lips almost parted. It is taboo for Shatong to show their teeth when not angry or aggressive. She pinned her lips together harder as her smile lit up her entire face. "I'll keep you posted honey. No problem at all!" The couple closed their respective view-ports at almost the same time.

The three young children began bouncing around their dad, "Who was that with Mommy just now?! Who was that?" Zomesh smiled at his kids as he got them ready to sit down for the lunch meal. "We'll find out together in due time. All in due time. Now eat your food."

Meanwhile, back on the carrier, Marshan fell into Toshang's arms crying uncontrollably. "The doc was right, I never should have gone. Death, death everywhere in Gronox territory! Ships looking like honeycombs coming straight for us! The girls (as she'd begun to affectionately refer to her little band of warriors) and I began to call them 'The Beast' for lack of a better term." Briefly straightening up with a hint of the former marksman and champion, Marshan declared, "but we won! Mop-up is complete! There is no more evidence of The Beast anywhere in Gronox space! No more children will die while they live. No more colonies turning to ashes. No more vegetation turned to piles of dust. NO MORE! NO MORE! No more. . ." Her voice trailed off as she collapsed into tears again.

Toshang helped her to her quarters and arranged for transport back to home world to resume reparative therapy. But before she boarded the ambulance pod, Toshang looked into her eyes and whispered, "We completed the trials Marshan. We completed the trials!" Marshan's tired green eyes brightened a bit as she realized that part of their coupling had indeed been completed. The circular doors spun shut as Toshang waved goodbye, longing for the day when the coupling could take place and they could live their lives in peace.

Several days later, a new entourage made their way to the Brig of the fourth carrier. Troops and personnel were mothballing the huge vessel and preparing to return to the planet as General Shanto, Admiral Toshan, Shateena and Commander Toshang once again stood before Gromin's cell. Several high-ranking researchers and medical doctors stood with them.

General Shanto addressed the young man. "Gromin, as you can tell by the buzz outside your cell, we are preparing to leave this ship and move back down to our home world. You are the only prisoner of war in our possession. As the only remaining member of your race, we wish to offer you asylum on our planet, free to roam as you please."

Gromin's eyes widened and he dropped a gift he'd been examining.

The General continued, "We have brought several doctors and researchers to meet you. If you so desire, they will be able to assess your

DNA, place you under surgery, and return you to your former self without the technological mess the Gronox left you with."

Gromin's gaze moved from the General to the others in the room. "You would be willing to remove all this. . . STUFF. . . and let me roam free on your planet??? Are you serious?" Gromin stretched out his arms, looking at the metal plates, tubes, and now-useless weapons permanently attached to him. "How exactly would you pull off that feat?!"

The various Shatong present all smiled back at him. One of the doctors spoke up next, "You prove your youthfulness by your questions young man. That encourages us as we are a race of brains."

"Three each to be exact" piped up one of the researchers. Gromin's eyes got progressively bigger.

The doctor continued, "We have biological technology that we have vowed no other race we meet will ever receive from our hand! We can use that technology to restore you, to learn about the kind of race you belonged to, and to ensure your life with us is a healthy one."

The group stood there anxiously awaiting the young man's response. Gromin sat down on the cot, pondering what it would be like to be whole again, among a race of beings he'd never seen till being captured. He liked the thought of being free, and figured if his life did nothing else, it would allow this race to learn of his race and put them in the history books for others to learn of in years to come. He nodded, stood up, and walked to the front of his cell.

"I will go with you."

It was the Shatong's turn to celebrate for the young man, knowing that his particular race would not be a complete and total write-off. Shateena stepped forward as the cheering died down, "Gromin, I have discussed this with my husband and with my remaining three children. We want you to become part of our family and take the place of Zolash at our table. You will be given his bed and all that was his will be yours."

Gromin's eyes got even bigger than they'd been earlier in this very strange turn of events. "Are you serious???"

Shateena and the others began to laugh, "Yes Gromin, I am quite serious." She beamed, holding out both her hands." Gromin hesitantly stepped forward as the others formed a circle around him and Shateena. He reached forward his own "hands" (remember one was a mere stub thanks to the Gronox cybernetic implants replacing it), but found himself involuntarily trying to hug Shateena instead. Now the sounds of celebration turned to empathetic displays as a tear escaped Shateena's eye and rolled down her face. She wrapped Gromin in a big soft hug and held him for a few minutes. Letting him go, she turned to one of the researchers.

"Yes, ma'am," He said out loud, "He will need to spend some time in our hospital's research centre so that we can do our best to return him to normal before you can take him home."

Shateena gave a single affirming nod, pretended to rough up Gromin's somewhat clear shoulder, and left the Brig.

CHAPTER EIGHT: TOSHANG

The months-long war had taken its toll on the Shatong people. Marshan spent several months in reparative therapy., a fair bit of that time in a med-pod Not far from her in the same facility, Gromin was starting to resemble a mildly heavy-set humanoid hedge-hog with full-sized arms, hands, legs and feet A growing pile of metal, rubber and plastic lay to one side of his room as the doctors and researchers worked. Scribes on site made copious notes of all that was found as the work progressed.

Toshang tried to busy himself back at his bachelor home. The plant-house had clearly missed him, and judging from its appearance when he returned, it had begun to pine away. Most Shatong think it's strange when a child runs out and hugs a tree, but one could forgive Toshang for feeling that same urge as he walked up to his neglected house. Shatong have a somewhat symbiotic relationship with their homes. As Shatong shed their protective and cleansing external slime layer while sleeping, the home absorbs this shedding, effectively eating or ingesting it for it's own growth and sustenance. Conversely, the home's exhaling of breathable air not only cleans the air around the home externally, but provides fresh air inside the home as well for its occupants. Not having Toshang home every night for the months it took to fight the Gronox war, caused the home to slowly begin starving.

Sure, the odd animal had clearly found its way through the spiral front doors, but their inability to control those doors meant they'd died. The home was able to gather bits of nutrients from these animals, but not enough to remain cheerful and strong.

Toshang set about cleaning the place, tossing out the few corpses that had found their way in, forcing the spiral door to stay open to change out the air inside, and initiate the home's cleansing cycle. The house, realizing its master was suddenly home, briefly went into overdrive, causing the soles of poor Toshang's feet to momentarily get stripped of their slime layer a little too forcefully! He smiled, went to a pillar in the home and gave his house a hug. It was good to be home.

Glancing outside, a child who had stopped to see what was going on, snickered and quickly moved out of sight. Toshang slowly closed the front door, went to his resting place and called up the bed to lay down. The home quickly responded as the rectangular raised platform rose out of the floor to knee-height. Knee-height to a male Shatong that is. As Toshang lowered himself onto the bed and laid down, he made a terrible realization. This would be the first time since the war began, that he could legitimately and fully rest! Suddenly he became painfully aware that for months now, he'd been running high, sleeping lightly, ever-vigilant and attentive to signals coming over the data waves. That high was coming down fast and if he closed his eyes, he'd get dizzy, feeling as if he was about to start spinning.

The home got concerned, as plants can, and did its best to accommodate by engaging in the slime layer cleansing process while Toshang lay awake. Maybe plants can't talk or communicate in ways sentients can understand with their ears, but science has proven that they do have feelings, do have social needs, and do care about those around them. Shatong homes, being the combination of biotechnology and plant matter, still show these same plant-type reactions. Toshang's home went one step further, tempering its excitement in an effort to bring peace to its inhabitant.

The home's efforts were not in vain as eventually, Toshang involuntarily nodded off into a long-overdue deep sleep.

He awoke well into the next day. The sun was already high in the sky when he emerged from his home to go hunt for breakfast. A mother with her young daughter slowly bounced past. Those large powerful thighs on female Shatong translate into bounding being easier for them than walking. This mother was teaching her young daughter how to move, taking a hop and then waiting for the young one to catch up. Thanks to being unsteady on her little legs, the young one at one point tried to balance herself too soon with her tail, causing herself to be flung to one side of the road. Mother laughed, helped her to her feet and the pair carried on.

Toshang smiled as he made his way to the outskirts of town to go find a meal. Sure, he could obtain it from The Hub in town. Not every Shatong had the time or energy before or after work to go hunting for themselves. Modern society for the past 1000 years had led to whole hunting industries springing up to feed the masses who worked in offices, research centres, and spawning pools. No, Toshang needed to head out into the forest for himself today.

He'd only gone a short way into the nearby forest when he spotted a pair of animal tracks. They appeared to duck under a bush and then reappear a short way up the trail, but not having irises, he couldn't see clearly much past that point. Everyone thought he was such a great hunter worthy of decoration in The Great Hunt every year, but all he ever did, was follow tracks and sounds. He was good at it however, so good that he generally got his quarry every single time. This particular hunt would have been largely uneventful, catching his prey and preparing to clean it, when the memories struck.

Six months or more of careful tracking of Gronox activity followed by the horrors of what he'd seen over that time came flooding back! He put his catch on the ground beside the log he'd sat down on. He couldn't look at it. How had he not had these feelings before? What had shielded him from the same raw shock and dismay that had sent Marshan and others into the med-pods?

Marshan. . . the love of his life. . . he could remember like it was yesterday, the day they joined their root saplings together to begin growing their marriage pod. She was beautiful!

That long slowly-twisting tail of hers rose gracefully behind her back and always seemed to have a flourish to it that captivated him. The glint that shone off the iris in her eye always made him smile no matter how he was feeling. The mental image made him smile now. All he could see was her. She was the reason he'd fought so hard and dove into his tactical maps so deeply. She was the reason he fought to spare their race. Now she lay in a med-pod, her fragile emotional state nearly destroyed by what she'd seen during this war. Her mental state having nearly collapsed at the sight of children. . . now it was his turn to burst into tears. Large drops of tears escaped from his oval orange eyes and crashed onto his knees as his muscled shoulders heaved with each sob.

Taloned feet dug into the earth as they curled up tightly in the same manner in which he was now balling up his taloned fists to pound the bark beside him. So many lost lives! So many lost planets! An entire race lost to the universe with who knows how many others swallowed up in its ruthless greed for expansion! Soon, anger replaced the tears! Ruthless greed is what had nearly wiped out the Shatong race centuries ago! Marshan had her history books mixed up, because the Progressives had actually created The Mother's Curse to unleash it on the Purists in an effort to wipe them out! But the progressives had failed to remember one key element of Shatong biology! A mutated Shatong will succumb easily to infections that might give a healthy Shatong the common cold, and then die. The Shatong biological make-up didn't then and wouldn't in the future, support short or long-term mutation without severe repercussions to those who engaged in it. The Progressives had been the ones to die out as a result. What Marshan had right, Toshang continued to muse, was the difficulty researchers were still having in identifying just which gene The Mother's Curse had affected, to stop it.

The time it took to muse about Marshan's misinformed memory of her history books subdued his anger and he turned back to his catch. Finishing the job of cleaning it and bringing it home for a quick marinade followed by a little singe-ing to eat, took the remainder of the noon hour. Soon, the familiar smells of noon dinner filled the little home, and Toshang's emotionally-spent body welcomed the food. He picked at it though, forcing himself to eat. For the first time in his life, and for the first time since the war, he was experiencing the beginnings of depression.

Two sets of teeth sunk into a drumstick as he realized that he too needed recovery time.

* * *

Shateena began making regular visits to the research centre at the hospital to learn of Gromin's progress. Her family was getting excited to have the young man join their household, and as the researchers uncovered bits of detail related to the young man's physiology, they began making preparations to accommodate. For example, while the Shatong are reptilian in nature, it became clear eventually, that Gromin's race seemed to resemble humanoid foxes. No, Gromin did not have a long snout, but it seemed as if there should have been a tail on there somewhere. The researchers still had to figure out key details. What they did learn was that he had a fair bit of hair all over him where palms, soles, face and neck were not involved. The hair seemed to be placed such that the concept of clothing wasn't necessary for his race either. Shatong were able to program instructions into their homes and offices so that pelts from hunting would not be damaged and could be used for display or for other purposes. Gromin's room would need to be instructed in a similar manner so that he could be cleansed every day but not destroyed by the home's ingestion of sweat, dust, and other impurities.

CHAPTER NINE: DESTROY THE BEAST!

"You're talking about research that SAVED LIVES!"

"You didn't see the devastation left behind!"

"And just who is going to tell our research centres and weapons techs that their hard work is going to be deliberately lost to history?! Huh?"

"We can't risk our race being wiped out again, nor that of any other race! If this technology gets into the wrong hands, even the wrong Shatong hands . . ." One Shoma sat down and buried his head in his hands.

"Yes even should we ever find corrupted members of our own race, this tech must NOT get into even THEIR hands!" Another Shoma finished off.

General Shanto's bright-blue eyes darted around the meeting chamber as the Shomadeen rose from her place. "Order! Order on the floor!" She shouted over the rising volume of both audible and signal-based arguments. Instantly there was silence.

Tension remained high however, as proponents of maintaining the technology stood against those who could not bear to see General Shanto's visual memories repeated.

General Shanto had been hauled before the Shomadeen when word of what happened in Gronox space had reached her. He stood there now, surrounded by sharp disagreement even worse than what he'd seen in the Shomadeer meeting aboard his carrier in the final days of the war. At that time, it took the advice of an elder to convince the High Governor to give the word to research and then use the weapon against its perpetrators. What no one in that meeting foresaw, was the utter devastation and annihilation it would cause in Gronox territory. General Shanto had been expected to explain his actions and their results. His presentation included Commander Marshan's findings on several planets, the findings from the covert away team, and the findings from the clean-up mission also headed by Commander Marshan, against Commander Toshang's better judgement and those of the doctors back on the home world. The images he shared over the local system had brought revulsion, tears, and clearly, passionate arguments as well!

All eyes turned to the Shomadeen now as she prepared to speak, surveying the room. What would she do with General Shanto? What would her consensus be regarding the technology that spared the Shatong race?

"Ladies and Gentlemen," Her strong booming voice filled the chamber, "We have heard General Shanto's testimony. We have seen the data feeds from those under him assigned to the tasks in his testimony. I understand the heated nature of this afternoon's discussion. . ."

Discussion??? Several councilmen shook their heads. Their top Shomadeer leader continued, "We do not have precedent in our history books nor in our books of law upon which to base today's decision. The initial purpose for which this new weapon was used was indeed achieved and would have earned General Shanto and his entire carrier our highest military honours. That is now severely tempered by the discovery that in saving our own race, those of another and potentially other races who had been swallowed up by them, were instead wiped out. The Gronox war ended in an exchange of one race's life for another, at the hands of this new weapon. Rumour has it this weapon was new for the Gronox as well, judging from some of the intercepted communications by General Shanto's men. Ordinarily, our law books would have a Shatong who wiped out another family, publicly shamed and then sent to the prison pods. General Shanto has not merely wiped out a single family, but an entire race!"

The silence in the room was now thick with consternation and emotion. General Shanto hung his head. The number of Shatong left in the Shatong empire was small when placed beside the loss of an entire race and potentially others they'd absorbed and assimilated. As he waited for the Shomadeen to strike the gong, he instinctively brought his hands together in front of him, he collapsed to his knees while closing his eyes, and awaited the verdict. It was true, an entire race's death now rested on his shoulders.

The Shomadeen lifted her tail above her bark-encrusted desk. Many Shomadeens had used this desk. It had stood for so long that it could no longer be pulled down into the floor of the chamber. In fact, every desk in the room now permanently stood in their places, evidence to the age of the Chamber and the building in which it stood. On the front of the Shomadeen's desk was carved the symbol of the Shatong Shomadeer. It had been painted the crest colours and those colours, applied so long ago, were now darkened stains of their former glory. The gong itself, was a membranous device carefully rimmed by carved wood, the same wood the building had grown from. The gong's membrane was polished and worn from centuries of use, having only been replaced once when the Shomadeen at the time snapped its skin while pronouncing the first and only death sentence of the instigator of The Progressives, ending the ancient Civil War. Hollow bone fragments were laid out in rows under the membranous skin, producing a loud snap when the membrane was struck. Needless to say, these bone fragments had received frequent replacements over the centuries.

"Men and women of this Shomadeer. What I am about to say will anger some of you and cause others of you to rejoice. What we can all agree on however, is that life must be protected AT. ALL. COSTS!"

51

She was interrupted by shouts of "Hear Hear!" Slamming her tail down on the gong, she regained control of the moment. "General Shanto took that mantra to heart, and we are here today to debate the merits of his decision! Don't let that escape the minds of a single person in this room! Because of General Shanto, we can stand here today and debate these issues! If we were wiped out, today's heated arguments would never have taken place!" Uneasy silence once again filled the chamber.

"Therefore my fellow Shomadeer leaders. I present a motion to preserve our race once and for all! All in favour of destroying any knowledge of the weapon that wiped out the Gronox, please stand, and in so standing, you show your desire to spare the Shatong any further similar threat in the future."

A solid third of the leaders on the floor stood immediately. As the Shomadeen waited, scattered Shatong here and there around the room began to stand. Slowly, more and more began to rise from their seats/squats, some grumbling that the only reason they were standing was for LIFE! The Shomadeen began to tap down the final seconds, indicating imminent closure of the motion. Eventually, only a handful of Shatong remained seated as her tail came down on the gong, its crack loud enough to be heard out in the adjoining hallways and offices.

"DONE!" She pronounced. "General Shanto, you may rise to your feet. Your life has been spared." Three Shatong began to loudly protest when she raised her hand for silence. "Only the heartless, only the selfish, only the self-serving and self-seeking would sentence their comrade to hell for saving their lives!" Three heads suddenly bowed in shame. Turning back to General Shanto, the Shomadeen continued, "General Shanto, your final task related to the atrocities of the Gronox war, is to personally oversee the destruction of this new weapon and everything related to it. You are dismissed from this meeting to attend to your duties."

General Shanto rose to his feet, nodded to the Shomadeen, and left the room to much cheering from those who were in favour of the decision.

Because the Shatong had wasted no time repopulating where they could, research centres once again dotted Shatong space, slowing down delivery and execution of the order.

Three privates were ordered to pilot the prototypes to a distant frozen planet only known to the navigator of the transport that would bring them back. Heavy equipment and operators travelled in the transport as well, with tug pods at the ready to lower the machines to the surface. The task took several days to complete before the prototypes were decommissioned, powered down, and buried. Upon arrival back at the home world, the navigator of the transport agreed to undergo minor databank recalibration to lock down knowledge of the completed mission's coordinates.

Never again, would The Beast be resurrected and used against another race. The Shatong Shomadeer instituted a period of mourning across the now shrunken Shatong space. Every system was to engage in this period of mourning for the prescribed time. After this period had passed, it was time for life as they knew it, to resume.

CHAPTER TEN: CELEBRATE!

Back on the home world, the time had finally come for Toshang and Marshan to be coupled. While most Shatong engaged in the coupling quietly, the populace wasn't going to let that happen to their decorated heroes! The day was celebrated with a stinger fly-past to celebrate Marshan's accomplishments, and last year's Great Hunt contestants provided a feast not seen since before the Gronox Wars began. Toshang's knowledge and ability to pinpoint prey in the Great Hunt was put to cheeky use, as Marshan hid until he successfully outlined her coordinates! Her previous coordinates we should add, as she sprung up behind him after the successful read-out to the delight of everyone present.

Indeed the day had been touched with much merriment, although murmurs could be heard wondering if Marshan's health would allow her to successfully become a mother. Her time spent in the medical pod had been beneficial for sure, her health having largely returned. But she tired quickly.

Seeing Marshan's efforts to hide her weariness, Toshang decided it was time to enter the marriage pod! The marriage pod had been growing ever since they'd touched down after that fateful battle, having been "started" by root saplings taken from their own homes before the war began. This had the added advantage of the pod being somewhat larger than normal thanks to the extra growth time made available to it while the Shatong fought off the Gronox.

It must be noted that normally, once the coupled Shatong enter the marriage pod, everyone goes home. One could liken time in the marriage pod for the Shatong as a type of one-night honeymoon. But life had taken a drastic turn for the Shatong. Many were still tense and living day to day on edge, wondering if the enemy would return and they'd all be wiped out. The cheering had subsided as our decorated heroes entered the marriage pod, but no one went home. Every single Shatong waited to hear if Marshan had conceived. Confusion quickly spread through the crowd when Marshan emerged unable to announce her conception. Rumours strengthened and got louder, wondering if the war had been too much for the Great Huntress. Toshang urged the crowds to find lodging in the city and a massive hotel located in one of the Shatong Trees (not to be confused with an actual tree, but a large living structure that housed many Shatong similar to the average home but with many levels, floors, and branches) opened their doors to the many visitors. Toshang plugged into the marriage pod, sending instructions to keep light roots going for the next while, to be ready for eventual planting at a more permanent location. He then took Marshan back to his former bachelor home to await word from the doctor.

It would take several days and even a return to the medical pod before Marshan finally made her way to the town square. Shatong in the streets sent the data waves buzzing and before Marshan even arrived at the festival platform, the square was filling up with a hopeful rainbow of scales and tails. She made her way to the centre of the platform before signalling to the sky with a flourish of her ample tail. As a second twist in her tail straightened, her trusted space aces suddenly appeared in small transports, dropping pink marinated bones down to the masses. Cries of delight erupted as various Shatong yelled out to each other, "It's a girl!!!"

Toshang held Marshan as she cried grateful tears of relief and joy! Her dream of becoming a mother had come to pass after all! The war had not rendered her victim to The Mother's Curse! She'd dodged another bullet, as the hunters are so prone to say when their prey get away on them. The Gronox had sought to wipe out the Shatong race but failed! Life would resume!

Her joy and tears were contagious as she shared her dreams with the masses. "The Shatong have NOT died! The Shatong have conquered! We will grow! We will multiply! We will teraform our space once more! But even more than that my fellow Shatong! Listen and listen well! We will expand BEYOND our former borders! We will bring LIFE to the death that lived in Gronox space! The child within me will do it! Your children will do it!" Marshan paused to catch her breath, her exuberance once again having caught up with her. Toshang stepped forward to end her speech for her with one final declaration, "Yes people! IT'S A GIRL!" The roar of celebration could be heard literally for miles as the tightly-packed towns, byways, hamlets, camp grounds, waysides and hillsides rang with wave after wave of celebration.

The Shatong in the few months since the battle ended, had begun dotting nearby systems with new research centres because bases had to be established from which teraforming operations could begin. Even this Shatong community spread across these nearby star systems, wished the new couple healthy hunting grounds as they set out to grow their own home and start a family.

Cutting loose the few roots the marriage pod had set down and boarding a transport, Toshang took his wife and unborn child into hyperspace on a new mission. They would be the first civilian residents of the Shatong planet that had held last year's Great Hunt. As the undisputed Champion of the Great Hunt for the past several years, Marshan wanted to make a statement to all Shatong everywhere, that THEY were the champions, the entire Shatong race, for having come through and lived!

Setting down on Netoosh in the Shinor System, Toshang poured over 10 month old logs to learn where the residential zones had been, where shops and businesses had been, and where the former research centre had been. He picked a spot where the marriage pod could grow into a healthy home for the family, and instructed it to set down a deep taproot. The pod, behaving as all plants do, discovered the rich soil created by the ash of those who had gone before, and began to grow with relish! The couple sent back word to the home planet to bring more settlers, this time with crop seed and cages filled with animals that used to live there. The teraforming would actually go faster than previously anticipated because of the nutrients that had been placed back into the soil.

Engineers arrived with tools to recreate the spawning pools that used to live in the industrial sector, speeding up the ability to create the needed tools to both teraform, clean, repopulate and return life to normal on Netoosh.

As Marshan looked out the translucent membrane of her home, she couldn't be happier. She would not enter in the Great Hunt next year, looking forward to standing on the sidelines with her baby girl, cheering on the next Shatong champion. Blackened spires of dead trees were being cut down, ground up and spread over the ground. Seedlings recreated from the DNA in the ashes were starting to take root, turning the ground into an amusing carpet of mottled greens.

CHAPTER ELEVEN: SHATEENA

Shateena set out for her usual daily visit to the hospital research centre that same day back on the home world. She and her husband had decided to stay on the home world and were quite happy with how their new home was responding to instructions to personalize it to their family's needs. Gromin's room was almost ready for him too, having been told to treat the room's contents similar to what a Shatong would need in preserving a pelt from hunting. As she entered the hospital and headed for the research wing, something felt different. Aides, nurses and custodial crews all seemed to eye her with a muted anticipation. Maybe she was just seeing things, so she kept on her way, picking up speed just a little.

She passed the research information desk with just a nod to the young lady who sat behind it. The staff there knew her now quite well, there was no need to check in anymore. Making her way to Gromin's room where he'd been moved a month ago, she paused at the doorway. It spiralled open as Gromin's nurse exited, almost running into Shateena.

"Oh hi!" The nurse greeted her. "Go on in, Ma'am. You'll like what you see today!" and the nurse hurried off.

Shateena watched her tail swish out of sight and then entered Gromin's room. A somewhat groggy, but quietly cheerful sight met her. Gromin was sitting up in bed, something he hadn't done since the reconstructive surgery had completed two months ago. He seemed amazed at himself, looking over his hands, arms, and feeling his head, neck and back of his shoulders. He looked up as Shateena approached.

"I can't believe you guys were able to do this!" Gromin exclaimed. "Look at me! I'm largely back to my normal self!"

Shateena squatted sideways near the bed so as to reach over and stroke the fur on Gromin's arm. "What do you mean "largely back to your normal self? Were our researchers not able to restore everything?"

"No, it's not that, your researchers are amazing! They just told me they couldn't remove what they were calling 'nano-bots' from my system. They've apparently never run into that technology before and don't know how to address it without upsetting my blood stream."

"Ah. How are you feeling today? You're actually sitting up for a change!"

"Yeah, I'm almost feeling back to my usual self. Can I come home yet? Am I doomed to be a lab rat forever???"

Shateena laughed. "Let me go talk with your nurse and see what he says." Gromin nodded as Shateena rose and left the room. Returning awhile later, Shateena was accompanied by the nurse, the doctor that had been assigned to him, and the head researcher. Gromin was to go through one more round of examinations and then he could go home. Gromin sighed, and was going to lay down to go limp for them when the nurse shook his head and told him to stay sitting up. What happened next would be quite familiar to human readers. Gromin's breathing was checked, then his heart rate followed by blood pressure, the "awwww" test with the tongue depressor, ear-checks, the whole thing. Even his reflexes were checked to be sure they were responding properly after reconstruction. A few more tests and double-checking of notes later, the doctor sent for an Aide.

"Young man, because you are not a reptilian race and instead a furry race, there are some things you will need to both observe and do in order to live successfully on our planet and in our society." The researcher began explaining. "First, you will need to carry a pair of special shoes with you everywhere you go. Each building you enter will have walls, flooring, tables, stands, beds, etc, much as you see in this room."

Gromin looked around the room more critically than he'd absentmindedly done for the past month or more since coming out of the restoration pod. "Everything looks part fleshy, part plant-like."

The researcher nodded, "You're partly right on both counts young man. I'd assume you are referring to the membranous surface of everything as "fleshy"? And the plant-like when observing the overall architecture of any structure you are looking at?" It was Gromin's turn to nod, his somewhat quizzical look urging the researcher on.

"We make heavy use of plant material in our building of homes and materials. Unlike plants however, these grow at our command as fast or as slowly as we see fit. I can tell your bed to disappear into the floor and it will, and tell it to rise up and it will. However, the walls and roof you see must be allowed to grow at their own pace according to specifications we have programmed. The strength of our buildings, tables, beds, etc comes from the type of material typically found in plant stems or tree trunks. Like all plants, our buildings need food to sustain themselves. This is where the membrane comes in that covers most surfaces, walls, etc. This membrane is responsible for taking the thin slime layer that covers Shatong bodies and absorbing it for food for the building.

Because you however, do not have such a slime layer, you must wear special shoes to protect your feet from accidental cleansing by whichever building you are in at any given time. You will even need to wear these at home. This might confuse you because we've let you touch the floor in this room without shoes a couple times. This room was programmed to treat you the way we have special compartments treat trophies from our hunts. We don't want pelts from our prey being destroyed, so we tell our buildings how to treat them. Your own room at home should be programmed to allow the same thing, correct?" The researcher turned to Shateena.

Shateena quickly nodded, "Yes, Zomesh has been busy programming and testing so that even the most delicate critter's pelt could lay on the floor overnight unharmed. Gromin will not need his shoes in his room. We are quite sure."

"Pelt! I'm being treated like a dead animal's pelt!" Gromin scowled looking out the translucent membrane near his bed.

For a moment there was an awkward silence in the room. Shateena began to get worried. She approached Gromin with a hand out-stretched. "Gromin, you must understand that we as a people have never met, much less interacted with someone from another race before. In fact, we thought we were going to get wiped out by the very first contact we made with another race. We can only do what we can with the knowledge we have to apply to your set of circumstances. As we learn more about your species, perhaps things will change more positively for you. But we want you to be safe among us and not die because of how we ourselves interact with our surroundings."

Gromin turned to her, his eyes and lips suggesting he was trying to understand and hold his peace. "So what else am I supposed to observe and do in your society?"

CHAPTER TWELVE: HOME

The aide returned with the shoes and the researcher bent down to make sure they fit. They resembled bark-covered clogs, for lack of a better description. The bark was intended to buffer his feet from pod and building membranes, while the membrane inside the shoe acted as a kind of soft, dry insole for the foot. Each shoe had been programmed to only accept whatever food came from the boy's sweat as outlined in his DNA. The spawning pool not far from the hospital had been instructed to pattern the shoes' cell structure and needs from desert-world flora and fauna.

While the researcher finished the fitting, the doctor continued, "You will also need a marking so that you are not mistaken for prey among us. We are meat-eaters, Gromin. A furry critter is generally seen as food. Should you be up and about before breakfast, and a sleepy Shatong happens to chance across you, we don't want you ending up on their plate!" Everyone gave a nervous laugh, including Gromin. "Therefore, you will wear this wrist band which contains a signal that any Shatong within range will pick up unless there is a wind storm. Your second marking will come from your family and be painted on your fur between your shoulder blades to mark you as a member of their household.

This will no doubt need reapplying every so often because your DNA says you will shed at times. Lastly, you must stay within city boundaries and within city parks only until our people are used to you being around, after which, you will be free to roam anywhere you wish. But until our people are used to interacting with a fellow sentient race that has fur instead of slime and scales, these limits are for your preservation."

Gromin nodded, glad that at least he could get out and stretch his legs. He stood up in his new shoes and grimaced slightly as the membrane formed around each foot. After standing there a moment, he tried to move forward and promptly buckled to the floor. "Oooh kay. . ." he muttered, "your planet's gravity is much higher than where I come from. . ." He tried to lift himself back up onto the bed, but the doctor had to help in the process. "My muscles feel weak." he said in the doctor's direction.

The doctor turned to the researcher, who upon reading the doctor's signals, explained, "That's because of not just our gravity level, but also due to how long you've been inactive while we restored you back to yourself. Your muscles honestly are weak. So you'll need to work out some form of exercise regimen when you get home, that will not only strengthen your muscles, but get your body used to the higher gravity here."

A few minutes later, and with further instructions for Shateena, the group helped Gromin out into the larger hallway. Shateena carefully brought around a portion of her tail behind Gromin's knees and gently pushed him off his feet. He fell onto her tail in surprise as her hand stopped him from falling backward. She smiled at his surprise. "Shall we go home now?" Gromin gave a tired smile in return and Shateena headed for the door.

"Before you go, Shateena!" The doctor said running behind her. Shateena stopped. "Gromin will need to return to receive his blood transfusion. We've discovered that if we replicate his own blood from his thigh bone DNA, we can flush out the nano-bots still left in his system!"

Shateena almost jumped for joy at the news as Gromin's eyes got big. "I will bring him back as soon as you have the transfusion ready! See Gromin, I told you we have amazing research teams!" Gromin's pleasure was overshadowed by his increasing weariness. "Let's get you home! The family can't wait to meet you!" She waved to the aide, researcher and doctor and left the hospital.

Outside, she positioned the rest of her tail to make a post of sorts on the other side of Gromin that she could hold onto as they walked. In this way, her body, tail and arm formed a kind of chair that Gromin found all too restful as they travelled. Rather than bound along as would normally be her habit, Shateena extended herself to full height and swung her legs forward to walk home. The rocking action only aided in further soothing Gromin's state of mind. They were half-way to the house when Shateena felt a thump against her side. Looking over, she found Gromin fast asleep. She let go of her tail and held him close for the remainder of the trip home, sending a signal on ahead that their guest was coming home already asleep.

Zomesh and the children raced into Gromin's room to put up the final touches. Shezoah, their daughter, insisted that a winter pelt be laid on the bed in case Gromin wanted a blanket. The boys brought in a welcome basket consisting of yummy marinated snack bones, home-made jerky (because the stuff at the local Dispensary didn't taste as good), and a hot cup of meat broth. When Zomesh was sure his programming was fine, (by checking Shezoah's winter pelt underside one more time), he herded the kids out of the room and over to the door. "Now remember children, Mommy says he fell asleep on the way here, so please don't wake him. We can all get to know him when he wakes up. You can watch as Mommy and Daddy get him into his room and into bed, but don't wake him, OK?"

Three Shatong children looked up at their dad with their trademark big eyes, three sets of hands clasped behind their backs as they positioned themselves to look but not touch. Satisfied, Zomesh opened the spiral doorway as Shateena came into view. Zomesh nearly burst out laughing as three throats began trying to squeal at seeing Momma bring home Gromin! Their joy over the data waves had passersby smiling too. Shateena beamed at her family, so proud to have such brave young

Shatong to raise and train. She led the tiny parade through the main room and into Gromin's room. With some careful positioning of her tail, she almost got Gromin onto his bed before he briefly woke up. But when he saw her smiling face, he drifted off again. Shezoah laid the winter pelt over Gromin and everyone crept out of the room.

As they sat at mealtime together that evening, the boys were full of questions about how Mommy found Gromin, what he looked like before, the stuff the researchers had to do, etc. Shezoah's budding youthful anger grew as she heard about the atrocities of the Gronox and what they did to Gromin. Seeing her young warrior's emotional temperature rising, Shateena paused in answering her sons' questions, "Shezoah my young girl, you are going to make a fine warrior in the Shatong peace forces one day. Your anger toward the Gronox is fully justified, but I must warn you, child. As awesome as our researchers are, they cannot and will not remove memories, thoughts, emotions, or anything that makes you who you are, and Gromin who he is. The Gronox used a chip to send directives into Gromin's brain. That chip is removed, and as a result, he is somewhat brain damaged. Therefore, if those directives get activated because of your anger toward the Gronox, you could get hurt."

Zomesh interrupted, "But you told us Gromin is not a Gronox! Should we all be wearing combat armour in case he tries to kill us???" Shateena looked sadly at her husband.

"No honey, but we do need to be mindful of what the Gronox did to Gromin so that we don't needlessly activate the programming they placed in his head. If that programming is never or rarely activated, then we know that it will eventually fade out. But if we deliberately behave in ways that activate it, there could be painful consequences to begin with until he gets the upper hand over those parts of brain activity."

Zomesh turned back to his food. Shezoah took a deep breath, looked at both parents and then returned to her food as well. Shateena would hardly get two more mouthfuls eaten before the boys were back at it, peppering her with questions.

*** Wrap-up ***

Toshang was the envy of his unit till the day he retired. It should be noted that not only had Marshan escaped The Mother's Curse, she was also able to assist other young mothers on Netoosh in spite of raising several children of her own. She became not just a prize hunter, marksman and fighter pilot, but an amazing mother at home as well. On the day their first child was born, an elder in the community publicly wished the couple many happy years and many generations to come.

Unbeknownst to Marshan, one of the young mothers she would assist, came from the rescue operation she'd conducted on the way home from Toshang's recon mission behind enemy lines during the war. This young lady had coupled with Goshan in the usual quiet ceremony featuring only close family and friends. Not merely being First Mate, but also having been long-time friends with Toshang, Goshan had answered the call for settlers to Netoosh and settled there within a month of the former couple's landing. Goshan and his wife were the proud parents of a boisterous, bouncing baby boy! Unfortunately for Neteesha, she could not create enough milk for the young one's healthy growth, so Marshan came alongside to offer assistance.

Yes, life was good now. Teraforming was going so well on Netoosh that the Shatong did something out of the ordinary yet again. Conception Day was declared in honour of Marshan's successful conception of a baby girl, and to remind the Shatong every year that they were not only NOT wiped out, but that clear permission remained to be fruitful and multiply, to grow and be creative, resourceful, productive, enterprising, and adventurous A race began to see which planet would be ready for The Great Hunt the soonest! Little by little, the home world began to breathe again as refugees returned to their former planets to assist in the teraforming with new pods for their families.

Out of the ashes rose a new generation of Shatong.

About the Author:

Welcome to the first fully-fictional work written by Author Marilynn Dawson.

Prior to this first book in what is to become a small series, Marilynn wrote mostly non-fictional works such as: "Becoming the Bride of Christ: A Personal Journey", "Mom's Little Black Book: Godly Advice for the High School Graduate", "Practical Thoughts on Becoming an Author", "Dressed for Eternity", "A Year in Prayer With Jesus","Pumpkin Pie From the Ground Up! (Well, sort of!)", "The Poor Man's Budget", "One Year Prayer Journal", ."Becoming the Bride of Christ: Study Journal", "30 Days of Advent Colouring Journal" and "Mom's Little Black Book of Skincare & Make-up" her latest non-fictional work released through Songdove Books, her own Imprint.

Marilynn is pleased to add her son, Isaiah Dawson, to her Songdove Books imprint as he commissions her to write his series on a science-fiction race he created, known as The Shatong, a young lizard-like space race.

Throughout her life, Marilynn has written poetry and published in the American Poetry Anthology(two issues). She has written numerous unpublished articles on end-time eschatology, written unpublished short stories, word studies and more.

Marilynn lives with her two grown children, cat, gerbil and two horses, in Kelowna BC Canada. Her day job sees her fix computers and engage in multimedia for her church. In the evenings and on weekends she's a soundtech doing various events through the year from funerals to workshops to concerts and weddings. Marilynn has sung alto or tenor in various choirs and praise teams over the years.

Marilynn can be contacted via her author page on Facebook at: https://www.facebook.com/Marilynn.Dawson.Author or by email: author@fa-ct.com